SmartGurlz

Adventures

Table of Contents

Chapter 1. Meet Jen

'Jen, it's dinner time, where are yooooou?' The question echoed throughout the seemingly empty autoshop. The room was littered with auto restoration equipment, scrappy paint buckets and piles of old tires. A vintage wooden desk stood covered in papers, brown dust and Coca-Cola bottles. Green wooden crates were filled to the brim with engine seals, gaskets, sockets, wrenches and screwdrivers.

Suddenly, a small, dirty face peered out from beneath a rusty, '67 Ford Mustang car.

'I'm here, Dad,' said Jen with a mischievous smile and a spark plug in her hand. The girl's real name was Jennifer Lee Samantha Davis, but everyone called her 'Jen'.

Red-haired, with a face lightly dusted with freckles, sixteen year old Jen was determined to take over her dad's struggling family autoshop one day.

Ever since she was little, Jen showed an intense interest in her father's work. Nearly 10 years ago, her dad inherited the '**Davis and Son Autoshop**' from his father, and Jen used to spend hours and hours watching her dad fix automobiles, motor scooters and even jet skis from the local boat club.

She loved the hustle and bustle of customers dropping off their vehicles and the thumping, whishing and whirling of the welding machines, drills and lifters in the garage. The pungent smell of gasoline lightly perfumed the air as the ceiling air filters pumped cool, fresh oxygen into the room. Music from a transistor radio blared out pop tunes, disguising some of the noise with its upbeat tones. Not bad for a local station, especially in Ann Arbor. Sunlight streamed through the filthy, soot-stained windows of the autoshop that served as Jen's second home.

As a youngster, Jen and her brother Jack were

'runners' at the garage, meaning they would bring all the tools her dad and the workers would need, and helped them however they could.

Sometimes Jack, along with being two years younger and five inches shorter, was a bit jealous of Jen, since she seemed to be a natural mechanic (better than he) and she was: 'gasp, a *girl*!'. Jack often teased his by calling her 'Jim' instead of Jen, and would snidely joke that she should go inside and learn to *'work'* the stove rather than hang about the autoshop.

'Hey, Jim,' Jack sneered, 'No man wants a wife who is covered in brake dust. If you continue hanging out here, you'll end up an old maid like Mrs. Butterworth.'

Jen would often get annoyed by her little brother's comments but instead of fighting back, she found briskly ignoring him usually worked. He would get bored and find another person to pester… or so she hoped.

'Move outta my way, Shorty.' said Jen as she lifted a battery pack over his head and into the open hood of a nearby car.

As Jen matured, her mechanical interests grew stronger, and her knowledge, deeper. Jen's curiosity knew no bounds. She would watch her father, mimicking his movements and begging her to show her how to fix things, or how to use the numerous electrical and mechanical tools in the autoshop.

By the time she started middle school, she knew the name of every tool on the autoshop floor. She even learned how to use many of them. By age 10, Jen was changing tires and had learned how to check and fill oil in the cars coming in for service.

Instead of spending time with her mom in the kitchen, learning to bake and cook as the other girls in the neighborhood would, she would spend the time with her dad in the garage at home or at the autoshop.

Even though she was still young, Jen began learning very quickly, and her curiosity about what was inside electrical objects bordered on the obsessive.

Jen's dad, Erik – wearing his usual work uniform of patch-covered khaki overalls and a backwards baseball cap – was always bursting to tell his customers about Jen and her latest electrical creation.

'My little girl Jen recovered an old toaster from the trash and converted it into a battery-operated S'mores machine,' He'd proudly claim, gesturing to Jen as she sat at the corner desk, busily working on her homework for the day.

'Wow, how she'd do that?,' asked one elderly, dark-haired gentleman. His bushy eyebrows creeped into his hairline as he spoke.

'She re-designed and flipped the toaster on its side so the chocolate could melt on the graham crackers and the marshmallows toasted lightly on the top. '

'Sounds really cool. If you produced those, I'd buy one for ym grandchildren!' declared another man.

Jen had entered her invention at the school science and engineering fair and won first prize: a shiny blue ribbon with gold threads and a painted medal embossed with a spanner on it.

Unfortunately, it wasn't long before Jack stole the S'mores toaster from his sister's bedroom and tried to make a marshmallow and ice cream sandwich, with disastrous results. The marshmallows were so close to the heat, that they ended up catching on fire! Luckily the ice cream melted and smothered the flames, but not without short-circuiting the machine as well. Jen's S'mores machine was stored in the attic.

After that day, Jen started to lock her bedroom

door. Determined to prevent this sort of thing from happening again, she posted a large sign as well: 'Do not Enter. Especially you, Jack.'

Her proud father would always say to her *"Jen, it would be a shame to waste a talent as fiery as yours in the autoshop. You can do more than just fix things – you can create things!"*.

Although her father's words stuck with Jen throughout her teenage years, she held on tightly to her hobby, and the dream that '**Davis & Son Autoshop'** would one day be changed to '**Davis & Daughter Autoshop'**.

Chapter 2: Who's That Girl?

Everyone at school knew Jen as an introvert, and a tomboy. She was always taking subjects like mathematics, physics, and chemistry, and generally kept to herself. She loved the finality of math, where the answer was either right or wrong – unlike in English or Creative writing where the answer was 'up for interpretation'. Jen would admit that she sometimes struggled in humanities classes, because it required her to write creatively. She would freeze up as she stared down at the blank piece of paper before her, frantically scouring her brain for the right words to appear, until she eventually worked herself into a panic and had to leave the room.

Her last written exam assignment about the American Civil War earned her a low grade of C minus, something which had Jen immediately crumbling the paper up and stashing it in her bag, hidden from view. Her mind briefly wandered to the prospect of college and the scholarships she would need to get there, before the thoughts were pushed firmly into the back of her mind.

But even though Jen was blossoming into a beautiful young woman, very little changed in her life. Every day she would return home, don her work clothes, and join her father in the autoshop. Sometimes he would inquire about her friends or boys in her life – the latter mentioned with the usual possessiveness of all protective dads – but Jen would always find a way to redirect the conversation or quietly dismiss the questions. She rarely brought friends over, and with good reason: She didn't really have any.

She could remember the last time she attempted to bring home a "friend". It was many years ago, in fourth grade that – at the urging of her mother – Jen invite a friend from class to come over. She hoped with all her heart that the classmate she brought with her – a friendly girl named Mary Beth – would find the **Davis and Son Autoshop** as thrilling as she did. Unfortunately, this was not the case. Rather than be excited, or even interested, the young friend was terrified and overwhelmed. As soon as she was back with her parents, she told them about how they had spent the afternoon in a "dirty, noisy, greasy garage" and that she never wanted to visit Jen again.

"Mary Beth, would you like to come to my house and play?"

"Your house? Last time, you invited me over, we spent the whole time in a boring, stinky garage "

"But it wasn't a garage, it was the autoshop!

"Whatever. You are a weird girl."

So instead of hanging with school friends at the

local park, Jen eventually started working as a technical assistant at her father's autoshop. Her father had been searching for a worker that would be able to help him out with all the work he had, and it didn't take much persuasion to have him agreeing that Jen would be the best choice.

Jen was delighted to work with her father, earning a bit of money and learning more about fixing and building cars. She didn't mind the dirtier aspects of the work: sticking her hand to her elbow in the motor oil, or going under the car to fix a brake, or messing with the exhaust. If it had wheels, she was happy to help with it.

After all the hard work and the successful year Jen had both at school and at work, Jen received a special present from her parents: a second-hand Segway-like electric scooter, something she had wanted to buy for herself 'for like forever'. It had been her dad's idea, although it honestly hadn't been too difficult to decide: Jen had been talking for months about how much she wanted a Segway, and complaining each time about how she could never seem to save enough money to buy one.

Not that she didn't try. She worked so hard at it, saving every penny she could and watching her spending. But she would always end up finding that gorgeous graphic t-shirt or that perfect pair of skinny jeans that she "just had to have", leaving her bank balance back at zero. Especially in the past few months, where her need for better clothes was becoming more than just a personal desire.

A new autoshop chain had recently opened in town, a place called Spiffy Lube. Their low-cost services rivaled even that of the family autoshop, and Jen's parents were forced to impose a strict budget on the family, including for clothing. Jen's cousins in

Florida, having heard about their dilemma, would send their old clothing to help cut-down costs. However, this posed two dilemmas: the clothes were designed for much warmer weather than would be found in Michigan, and Jen was taller than her cousins, especially in the arms. So, she would find herself piling on layers just to stay warm, something which didn't go unnoticed by the other, more fashion-conscious girls at school, as shown by their spiteful Facebook comments.

'*Oh look, here comes Jen dressed for Halloween as Orphan Annie.*' One commented on a picture Jen had posted of herself. Soon, others joined in:

'*Want to go shopping this weekend? I heard the dumpster at the Red Cross is having a sale – buy nothing and get one free!*' Another mocked.

'*Hey guys, come on, don't be mean – Jen can't help if she's got the fashion sense of a colorblind hobo.*' That one got several "likes".

'I bet she doesn't even shop at Goodwill – just digs through their rejects!'

The comments had hurt, and for a time Jen swore she'd never return to school again. But then her mother took her aside, and gave her some advice.

'You have never let the words of others stop you from being yourself before. Don't let the ugly words of some mar the true beauty of yourself."

Chapter 3: Surprise!

It had taken some time, and Jen had had to endure the biting words and sideways glances for a while longer. Now though, months later, when the autoshop was doing better, and she was jumping excitedly around the freshly-polished Segway in the middle of the garage, she realized it was all completely worth it. She walked up the motorized scooter, taking in the shiny matte black color and the gazing in awe at the beautiful red ribbons which decorated its surface. Her father, never missing a chance at praise, spoke up.

"Consider this part of my thanks for all your hard work, at school and at work. I wouldn't have been able to keep the autoshop running without you, Jen, and I couldn't be more proud." Jen's vision began to blur as happy tears formed in her eyes, and she darted over to hug him and her mother. As the hug ended, Erik eyes suddenly widened.

"I almost forgot. Go turn it on." At Jen's questioning look, he laughed. "It's part of the surprise. Go on."

Jen switched on the scooter, and was almost immediately started by a beautiful, neon red light which emanated from underneath it. Surprised, she looked to her father, who smiled proudly.

"I installed the lights myself. Do you like it?"

"Like it?" Jen leapt into his arms once more, hugging tightly. "I love it! Thank you both so much!"

From the moment Jen got her Segway, she started learning how to fix it on her own. Knowing only how to do a few minor repairs, Jen often found herself asking her father for help. Not that she minded – her father had been her mentor almost all of her life, and with all the riding she did to school and around the neighborhood and town – enjoying how the wind blew through her strawberry-blonde hair – she was learning how to fix something new every week.

She was starting to make a few friends in school, too. Once the word got spread about Jen's ability to brilliantly fix Segways, other students with Segways and electric scooters started coming to her for help and advice. She became the school's most trusted mechanical engineer, as well as earning a bit of extra cash on the side.

The change wasn't without it's bumps, however. As the weeks were passing by, Jen was getting closer to the day that her response from N.I.T – her dream college – would arrive. All the school presentations and other students talking about college – where they would go or want to go, what they wanted to study – was making Jen nervous. She had decided a long time ago where she would go and what she would study, so there was no thinking about that. But there was something else that was bothering Jen, something she hadn't heard mentioned amongst the others, and it was starting to tear her apart from the inside. She went to the student counselor with this problem. She explained,

"One of the happiest moments of my life might also to be one of the saddest and most heartbreaking ones. I know that going away for college means leaving my home, my dream job, and most important of all: my favorite person in the whole world and my best friend, my dad. I don't know what to do. I can't decide. Instead of going this year, I could stay, work with my dad and not go to college, or I could go next year."

The counselor said "Jen, I work with many students and have heard many problems. This is a common one. Many students struggle to leave home and go somewhere for four years. I'll tell you what I tell all of them: Go to college. It is a crisis phase and you will get past it. If you don't go, you will regret it the rest of your life." Jen left the student counselor's office and went home, the grave words echoing in the recesses of her mind.

Almost every night, Jen would toss and turn feverishly in her single bed, unable to sleep and overwhelmed by the stressful thoughts constantly running through her mind. Every day the covers would end up crumpled on the floor, and her pillow squeezed into a ball as a result of her frustrations. She knew that if she left, she would no longer be able to see her dad every day, and work with him at the autoshop. Jen appreciated those father-daughter moments and the time they spent together was more precious to her than words could describe.

Jen returned to spending more time at the

autoshop with her dad, knowing that their time together was going to be shorted all too soon. Erik noticed Jen's sadness and thought long and hard about how he could cheer her up, before finally coming up with a surprise.

One day, as Jen was getting ready for school, her dad knocked on her door.

"Come in." Jen called. Erik entered the room, smiling in an odd way, as if he was trying not to seem too happy.

"I need to borrow your Segway for some things at work. Do you think you can walk or maybe catch the bus to school?"

"Okay." A little confused, but always happy to help her dad, Jen agreed.

Once Jen had left for school, Erik took her Segway and locked himself in the garage. He would come out from time to time, only to something from the house and go back in. A little before Jen came from school, he left for the autoshop. When Jen finally arrived home, she looked for her dad – but he was nowhere to be found. She tried looking in the garage, only to find the doors locked tight, preventing her from entering. Just as she was about to give up, Jen heard the front door open, and her father rushed inside. He breezed past his daughter and unlocked the doors to the garage, quickly entering before Jen could ask him what was going on. Music began blaring from a radio almost immediately, covering any other noise from within. Strange. Any questions she had in regards to his odd behavior, however, quickly disappeared once she caught sight of what was on side-table in the living room: a big white envelope, stamped with the bright logo of N.I.T. and her name.

For a moment, Jen couldn't breathe. Anxiety

churned within her stomach, twisting her stomach
into a sickening knot as a cool sweat dampened her
face and neck. And yet, deep within the chaotic
emotion, she felt a twinge of something else:
excitement. Tingling, electric tendrils that sent a wave
of goosebumps forming over her skin, her entire body
dizzy with energy. She knew she was what they were
looking for. Years of struggle flashed before her
mind's eye: long nights spent studying, pacing about
her room as the blank writing assignment glared
accusingly at her from the desk, the advanced classes
and crippling exams she'd forced herself to conquer
(knowing all too well that merely "drifting about"
wasn't good enough for college), and the resume
where she'd proudly talked about her time outside
school, spent working in the autoshop and doing
mechanical work for the other students. Yet, a single,
dark moment broke through: Her history final. The
hated, torturous test that she'd passed by the skin of

her teeth, and what may very well serve as the spark
which sent all that hard work up in flames.

Chapter 4: The Letter

Hands shaking, Jen practically ripped open the envelope, silently sending up a prayer as she withdrew the papers from within.

'Please, please, please tell me I've been accepted! I won't ask for anything else, just let me have this!'

Taking a deep breath, she focused, her eyes scanning the words as quickly as she possibly could whilst still making out the words. Her heart dropped – there it was.

'Dear Miss Davis,

Congratulations! It is our pleasure to announce that you have been accepted as a potential student for N.I.T this coming semester.'

One little sentence, and yet those words had Jen

immediately leaping into the air. Her elated cries pierced the air – "Yes! Yes! Yes!" – and she almost immediately began calling for her father, her mother, Jack, eager to announce the great news. Alas, her father was still busily working in the garage, and nobody else was home, so Jen returned to reading the letter, a delightful grin planted firmly on her face…only to slowly slip away as she neared the bottom of the page.

'Your commitment to pursuing your goals and achieving personal excellence has convinced us that you will both improve yourself within our academic environment and contribute to our community. We think that you and N.I.T. are a great match.

However, while we are pleased to offer you a place at our esteemed school, due to competitive applicant pools we regretfully are unable to offer you a scholarship or financial aid at this time.'

Jen's heart dropped like a stone. No financial aid. No scholarship. How was she going to afford tuition? Legs suddenly unable to support her, Jen collapsed bonelessly into a nearby chair. She was going to throw up. No, she decided, feeling a warm, wet sensation streak her cheeks. She was going to cry first, and *then* she was going to throw up.

"Jen! Jen can you come in here?" Erik called. Wiping her eyes, Jen started walking toward the garage.

'I'll have to tell him what happened.' She decided, striding firmly into the other room. *'He's going to find out eventually, when I don't start packing –'* Her thoughts stopped dead with her footsteps.

"Surprise!" Erik stood proudly in the middle of the garage, right beside her Segway. Or better put, **parts** of her Segway. Bits and pieces of machinery lay strewn about on the floor at his feet. The scooter was missing a wheel, and the handlebars rested on a nearby toolbox.

"Wh-What's going on?" Jen managed, shock clear on her face.

"I took apart your Segway, and bought some new parts for it. I thought… we could build an upgraded version of it. Faster and better than the old one." He explained, his expression hopeful.

The thought of working on a project together with her dad eased some of the pressure on her heart, and Jen smiled brightly. This was *exactly* what she needed right now. Noticing her expression with a grin of his own, Erik reached back and tossed Jen her work clothes.

"Come on, there's plenty of work to do!"

Jen went inside and got changed in near-record time, eagerly picking up and examining each new piece she came across. The shine and feel of the brand-new parts sent an excited thrill through her spine, and a bubbling laugh escaped her lips. They set to work immediately, side-by-side, and getting lost in the familiarity of the work. It was just as they were replacing the handlebars of the Segway that Jen remembered the letter she'd received.

"I almost forgot to tell you; I received a letter from N.I.T. today." said Jen. Her dad looked at her, excitement clearly shining through his gaze.

"And? What did they say?"

"Well… They have good news and bad news. They said I was a talented student, a great match for their community, and…" Jen paused for as long as possible, "that I have been accepted."

Erik practically scooped up his adult daughter, an enormous grin on his face and a proud mistiness in his eyes. Jen laughed, delighted by the affection.

"That's wonderful news!" He set her down, warm hands resting heavily on her shoulders. "I'm so proud of you, Jen. You're going to do wonderful in life, I just know it."

Jen smiled and hugged her dad again, trying to hide the tears that suddenly formed from his view.

'There's no arguing it, now. I have to find a way to pay for school, I just have to!' She firmly decided.

The next day, Jen still had no idea how she was going to afford tuition. She had spent most of the night tossing restlessly back and forth, her mind flooded with haunting images of college and a towering pile of tuition bills. She even began her early morning searching for potential scholarships online – page after page of potential options and offers – but her efforts were fruitless. The few she could apply for, called for an essay – which she was unlikely to come up first in – and the others, weren't accepted by

N.I.T.. She was running out of ideas. More importantly, she was running out of time. A knock on the door interrupted her work.

"Come in!" She called. Her father stuck his head into the room, smiling.

"Hey, kiddo, what are you up to?" Jen quickly closed out of the scholarship sites, turning her chair to face him.

"Just looking up what I'll need for my classes." She lied. Erik came in and sat on the edge of her bed beside her. He was quiet a moment, looking about her room – the walls nearly covered in mechanical designs and logos for N.I.T., her desk (a smaller version of the one which sat in the autoshop, upon her request years ago), and the same purple bedspread she'd had (and loved) since he bought it for her birthday - as if trying to memorize everything which sat there. Like he was seeing it for the last time.

"What am I going to do without my favorite girl?" He shook his head softly, then looked at Jen, his voice wavering a bit. "I'll miss you so much honey."

"I know, dad. I'll miss you more." Jen's heart clenched, her eyes growing wet. God, she couldn't even *talk* about going to college without crying! Erik rubbed at his eyes.

"All right, let's stop crying. This is important. You promise me that you will call every day, and that you will take care of yourself, okay?"

"I promise dad. I will call every day, and I will tell you all about everything that happened. I'll even video call you, and we can even fix some things together." Jen said, wiping the tears from her face.

"All right." Erik smiled once more, and stood up, offering a hand to his daughter. "Come on, let's go get some ice cream. My treat."

"Okay." Jen took his hand, smiling back. Ice cream had often been her father's solution to a bad day, when she was a kid and even working in the autoshop couldn't cheer her up.

After a quick visit to the local ice cream shop, Erik drove the pair to a nearby lake. A quiet spot, treasured by the locals, people would often come by here to fish or enjoy the serene atmosphere. A volunteer group had made the area their "project" one year, and had convinced several local businesses to donate toward putting in wooden benches, including '**Davis and Son Autoshop**'. It was on this particular bench that they sat now, the small, faded bronze plaque showing gratitude for their contribution. Leaning back, Jen's father sighed contentedly.

"I could happily sit here with you for the rest of my life, kiddo. All these years, working together in the autoshop, watching you and your brother grow up – this is every parent's dream. It's my dream, and it makes me happy that things turned out this way. I hope you find your dream too, kiddo. This is the most important part of your life for it, after all."

"Don't talk like that dad, or I won't have the strength to leave you and Mom. I know that she'll cry her heart out, so I need you to be the strong one, okay? It's not the end of the world. I will come back often, and you can come and visit me. Who knows, maybe one day we'll open a big auto repair shop and grow it into a chain. Then I will be all over you about all the expenses, and how you need to work more." Jen said, the both of them falling into laughter at the thought. They finished off their ice cream, and made their way down to the shore of the lake, walking along the water's edge.

"Dad, I'm a little bit scared. I come from a small

town and will go to one of the biggest cities in the world, and will have to compete with many people. I won't know anyone at N.I.T.. What if I don't find any friends? Or what if I am the stupidest student there. We hear about prodigies on the news every day, what if they go there?" Or if I don't find a way to pay in time, her mind unhelpfully added.

"Calm down, Jen. Everything will be fine, don't worry about it. You have been one of the best in your school ever since you started going there. When you go there, don't let your guard down. Even though you may feel shy or scared, don't let them see that. Act strong and walk in with your head held high. They are not better than you. You are thinking that now, but in fact, when you go there, you will see a lot of kids that are terrified of being there. You are not the only one." Erik told her. Jen took a deep breath.

"Okay dad. Thanks. I'm not saying I won't be

scared or nervous, but I'll try to remember what you said now. Will you and Mom go to New York with me?" She asked hopefully.

"Yes, of course Jen. We'll help you settle, and then we'll be on our way." Her father stopped and checked his watch. "Let's go home now, your mother must be worried." Jen nodded, and followed him back to the car, empowered by the knowledge that amidst all the problems, she at least had the comfort of knowing her dad would be there if and when she was finally off to college.

Chapter 5: Goodbye

Jen never got that chance. That same night, after they got home, her father returned to the autoshop with Jen to work on the Segway some more. He had been joking about her having "the baddest scooter on campus" while reaching for a screwdriver…and collapsed, not waking up again. Jen had run inside, screaming for her mother and calling 911, but by the time the EMTs got there, they said it was too late.

A ruptured aneurysm, the doctor called it. No symptoms, no pain, no time. Just… death.

"He likely didn't even realize what was happening." The information provided very little, bittersweet comfort. The family was devastated, and Jen found herself spending most of her days in her room, alternating between violently sobbing into her pillow, her body wracked with agonizing pain – and simply staring blankly at the walls. Sometimes she would slip into a state of denial. Her father wasn't dead, he was just out buying parts. Any minute now, he would return, eager to show Jen the new addition for her Segway and telling her that it was time to get back to work. But he never did. Erik was gone, forever.

The funeral took place a few weeks later. Friends of the family and former customers showed up to pay their respects, all garbed in black and many with bloodshot, dripping eyes. As the casket was lowered into the ground, Jen could hear several people begin sobbing, a few crying out at the unfairness of it all. Jen's mother remained silent at her side, eyes locked on her husband's grave and cheeks damp, determined to be strong for her children. Dozens of people walked up to them after the service to hug them, to offer kind words about Erik and how if they needed anything, they could turn to them. Jen's mother thanked them, but Jen said nothing, listlessly staring at the ground as if everything that was happening was just a horrible, twisted dream.

She couldn't sleep that night. Jen stared at the ceiling, the walls, and the posters, tendrils of pain squeezing at her chest with each familiar sight. Then her eyes fell on her computer. Slowly, almost zombie-like in her stride, she got up and stumbled over to the desk, collapsing in her chair. For a few minutes she only stared at the screen, unsure what to do. Then she opened a new window, ignoring the offered links to scholarship sites and Facebook, and typed in an old address, blinking at the bright screen which popped up: '**Jen and the Art of Motor Scooter Maintenance**'.

She had started the blog years ago, when she was eight, under a different name, though the address had yet to change. She'd found that when a project didn't go as planned, or when she was having a particularly frustrating day, she could write about all that had happened, and start to feel better. She would even write about happier days, and look back on the entries – and as she got older, the comments as well – when she needed cheering up. She'd stop writing in a few years ago, having become too busy with school and work at the autoshop, but now… Setting her hands numbly on the keyboard, Jen began to type, gradually increasing in speed until her fingers practically flew across the keys.

"Well… Hello there, dear readers. Or rather, what's left of you. It's been a while since I've written on here, hasn't it? A lot has certainly happened since then.

Have any of you ever lost someone you really cared about? Maybe it was your favorite pet, or a grandparent, or that best friend you had all throughout primary school. Do you remember what it felt like to lose them? I do. Because recently, I lost my dad.

It's weird, thinking about how he's gone. And sad. And painful. He was so happy when I told him about me getting accepted into N.I.T. and I never got the chance to tell him the truth: that I didn't get a scholarship, or financial aid, so I might not go at all. He was so excited, and kept telling me how proud he was, that all of this was a dream to him. I don't know what to do. Without Dad there, the autoshop feels empty. Almost...lifeless.

Mom told me we can't afford to keep 'Davis and Son Autoshop' open any longer. I told her I'd stay, work every day if I had to, but she insisted college was more important. Confession time. Mom was quiet for a long while, then said "We'll find a way." Before going to her room. Her room... not "theirs" anymore.

Here's hoping something changes soon. I can't stop crying.

Forever yours,

Jen

Chapter 6: Friends in Cyberspace

The next day, Jen was surprised to find people had already begun to comment on her blog post. Encouraging words were found on every page:

'So sorry for your loss. That's really horrible. ;(Keep your head up, Jen!' –JazzyGirl99

'Don't give up just yet! I'm sure you'll find a way!' –Ottomatic64

'Prayers and love coming your way. Congrats on your acceptance, and so sorry about your dad. ☺ –Jsmithson

A knock echoed from her door, and Jen's mother entered the room before she could respond.

"Sweetie, I have something important to tell you." Jen got up and sat next to her mother on the bed. Her mother looked as if she had aged twenty years since the funeral, and shadows stood out boldly beneath her eyes.

"I just got off the phone with our insurance company. You'll have to get a job, and it'll be a close call with orientation… but your father's life insurance will cover tuition for this semester." She explained. Jen was in shock.

"I…I don't know what to say." Her mother grasped her hand, looking at her with a solemn gaze.

"You weren't the only one with a dream of going to college. Your father would want you to do this." Slowly, Jen nodded in agreement.

In the time between then and orientation at N.I.T., Jen took advantage of the time she had left with the autoshop and finished working on her Segway. When the day finally came to leave for New York City, Jen's mother and her brother were with her. They got settled in, and Jen took the opportunity to explore the city. It was bigger than anything she'd ever seen. She wished she had her Segway, but her mother had been quick to point out that such a bulky device likely wouldn't fit into a dorm, and wouldn't be allowed on the plane. Jack promised to take good care of it – Jen could only hope that meant he wouldn't touch it!

Jack and her mother remained in the city for a few days, just long enough for her to go through orientation and get settled into her dorm. Tearful goodbyes and hugs were exchanged at the airport, and as Jen watched their plane disappear into the sky, she thought of how she wished they could stay, and that her dad could be there to see her now. Still, she knew he would be proud if he was. She had finally made it.

A few days later, Jen decided to update her blog once more:

"Dear blog-readers

I've been wanting to sit down and update you on the important moments of my life lately, but going to college took a big toll on me.

The first couple of days were a struggle for me. I had to leave my home, leave my mother behind and be separated from her by hundreds of miles. I'm talking to her every night, video chatting with her, but it's just not the same.

Overcoming the part where I was homesick was hard, but then the interesting things started happening here on campus. N.I.T. is even better than I imagined. The library is enormous, the laboratories are fully equipped, and frankly, I can't wait to start my Physics class. There are all sorts of clubs, even one for mechanical engineering! You can be certain that I'll be looking into that soon.

At first, I felt like I was lost in another universe. I

was bumping into people, and looking at my phone, trying to find the main amphitheater where the speech was held. I felt completely lost, like I didn't belong here. I think, for a moment, I even doubted coming here. But then, things started changing. After the tour around campus, I overheard Maria, a girl that wants to study aerospace engineering, talking to Jim, the mechanical engineering guy. Something about hot-wiring cars. I immediately thought "That's my thing!". I joined their conversation and explained to Maria, step by step, how it goes. She was impressed by how much I know about machines, so we started talking, and we found out we shared a lot of the same interests. We walked around, when we overheard Cecelia and Jun, two shy girls, talking how they were nervous about making friends. Maria turned to me and said she felt the same. We approached Jun and Cecelia, and all together went to have lunch at the cafeteria. We ended up having a wonderful afternoon together.

I have to stop here, to get started on my classwork and start looking for a job. I hope you are looking forward to, as much as I am, all my new adventures at N.I.T.

Truly yours,

Jen xx

Made in the USA
San Bernardino, CA
13 January 2020